KU-008-330

MR.MEN **LITTLE MISS**

MR. MEN and LITTLE MISS™ © THOIP (a Chorion Company)

www.mrmen.com

Mr. Men and Little Miss™ Text and illustrations
© 2010 THOIP (a Chorion company).
Printed and published under licence from
Price Stern Sloan, Inc., Los Angeles.

Original creation by Roger Hargreaves
Illustrated by Adam Hargreaves
First published in Great Britain 1998
This edition published in Great Britain in 2010 by Dean,
an imprint of Egmont UK Limited
239 Kensington High Street, London W8 6SA

Printed in Italy
ISBN 978 0 6035 6573 1

1 3 5 7 9 10 8 6 4 2

LITTLE MISS NAUGHTY
WORRIES
MR. WORRY

Roger Hargreaves

DEAN

Little Miss Naughty is quite the naughtiest person that I know.

Take the other day for example.

She tied Mr Tall's shoelaces together.

And she took Mr Dizzy into the
maze and left him there.

And she joined up all the dots on
Miss Dotty's house.

And she even picked on the worm
who lives at the bottom of her garden!

I think you would have to agree that she is probably the naughtiest person you know.

Then one day Little Miss Naughty met Mr Worry.

Now, Mr Worry is the sort of person who worries about everything.

Absolutely everything!

"Let's have some fun," suggested Miss Naughty, after they had introduced themselves.

Mr Worry was worried that if he said no he might offend Miss Naughty, so he said yes.

But he was still worried what 'fun' somebody called Miss Naughty might get up to.

And as you have seen he was right to worry!

Miss Naughty led him to Mr Tickle's house.

"Let's ring Mr Tickle's doorbell and run away," she giggled.

"Ooh, I don't know," said Mr Worry. "Mr Tickle might be in the bath."

"Even better!" laughed Miss Naughty.

"But then he would be all wet, and he might slip, and he might fall down the stairs, and he might bump his head, and then there wouldn't be anybody to call the doctor because we would have run away!"

Up to this point Little Miss Naughty had never worried about anything in her entire life.

But now, when she thought about what Mr Worry had said, ringing Mr Tickle's doorbell and running away suddenly didn't seem such a good idea after all.

"Come on," she said. "I've got a
better idea."

They walked over to Mr Uppity's house.

"Why don't we let his tyres down?" chuckled Little Miss Naughty.

Mr Worry looked worried.

"But what if Mr Uppity didn't notice he had flat tyres until he got out on the road, and then he might get stuck, and then a fire engine might come along, and it might not be able to get past, and then it couldn't put out the fire!" gasped Mr Worry.

"Oh," said Miss Naughty. "I hadn't thought of that."

She had thought of something else though, and off they went.

But it didn't matter what she thought up, Mr Worry could think of something to worry about. Which then gave Little Miss Naughty something to worry about.

They didn't push Mr Bounce off the gate because he might have bounced up into a tree and never been able to get down.

They didn't scatter Little Miss Scatterbrain's marbles because she might have got upset if they had been lost.

Little Miss Naughty was distraught.

All those wonderful, naughty ideas
going to waste.

And then she had another idea.

And tripped up Mr Worry who fell
flat on his face!

"What did you do that for?"
said Mr Worry.

"I might have rolled down the hill,
and I might have fallen in the river,
and then I might have caught a cold,
and I might have had to stay in bed
all week!"

Little Miss Naughty looked at Mr Worry.

"But you didn't," she said, and ran off giggling mischievously.